Date: 6/18/24

**PALM BEACH COUNTY
LIBRARY SYSTEM**

**3650 Summit Boulevard
West Palm Beach, FL 33406**

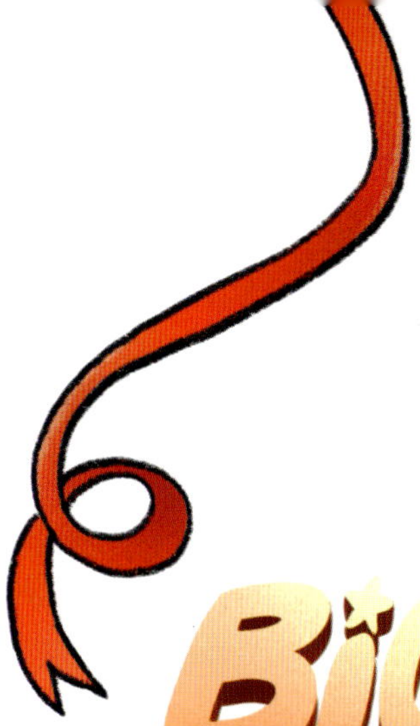

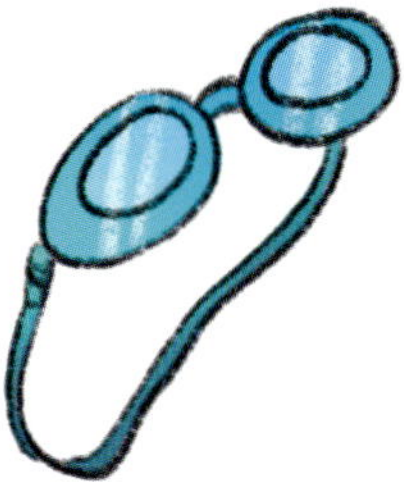

BIG SISTER COCO

THE BIRTHDAY SURPRISE

Story by
Jesse Byrd

Illustrations by
Lau Moraiti

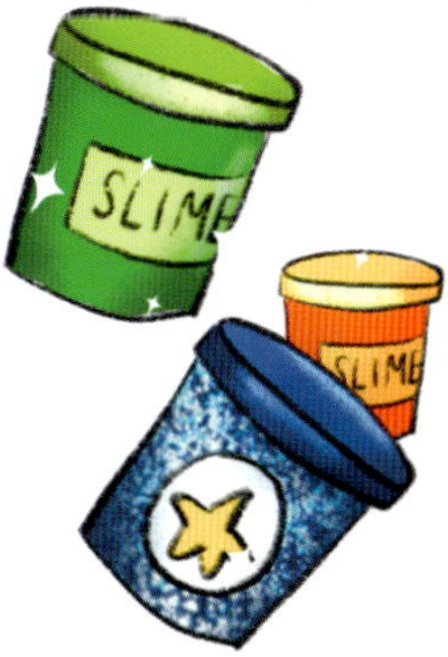

SLIME
SLIME

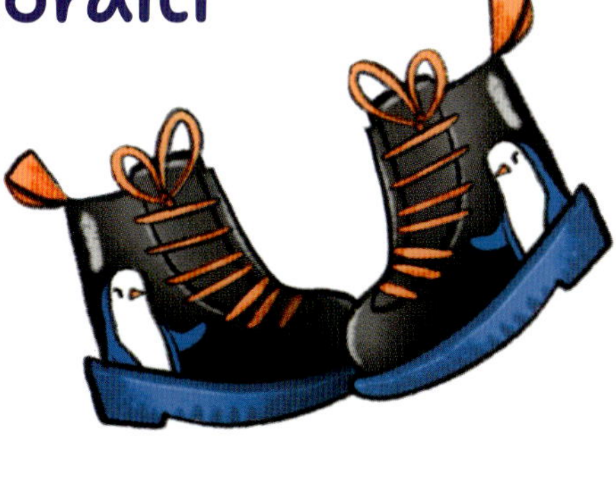

To my little brother, Isaiah
—Jesse

To my loves, who inspire
me to chase my dreams
—Lau

Book and Cover Design by Lau Moraiti
9781223187075 Hardcover English
9781223187082 Paperback English

Published by Paw Prints Publishing
PawPrintsPublishing.com
Printed in China

PAW PRINTS
PUBLISHING

1.

Where Is Bo's Present?

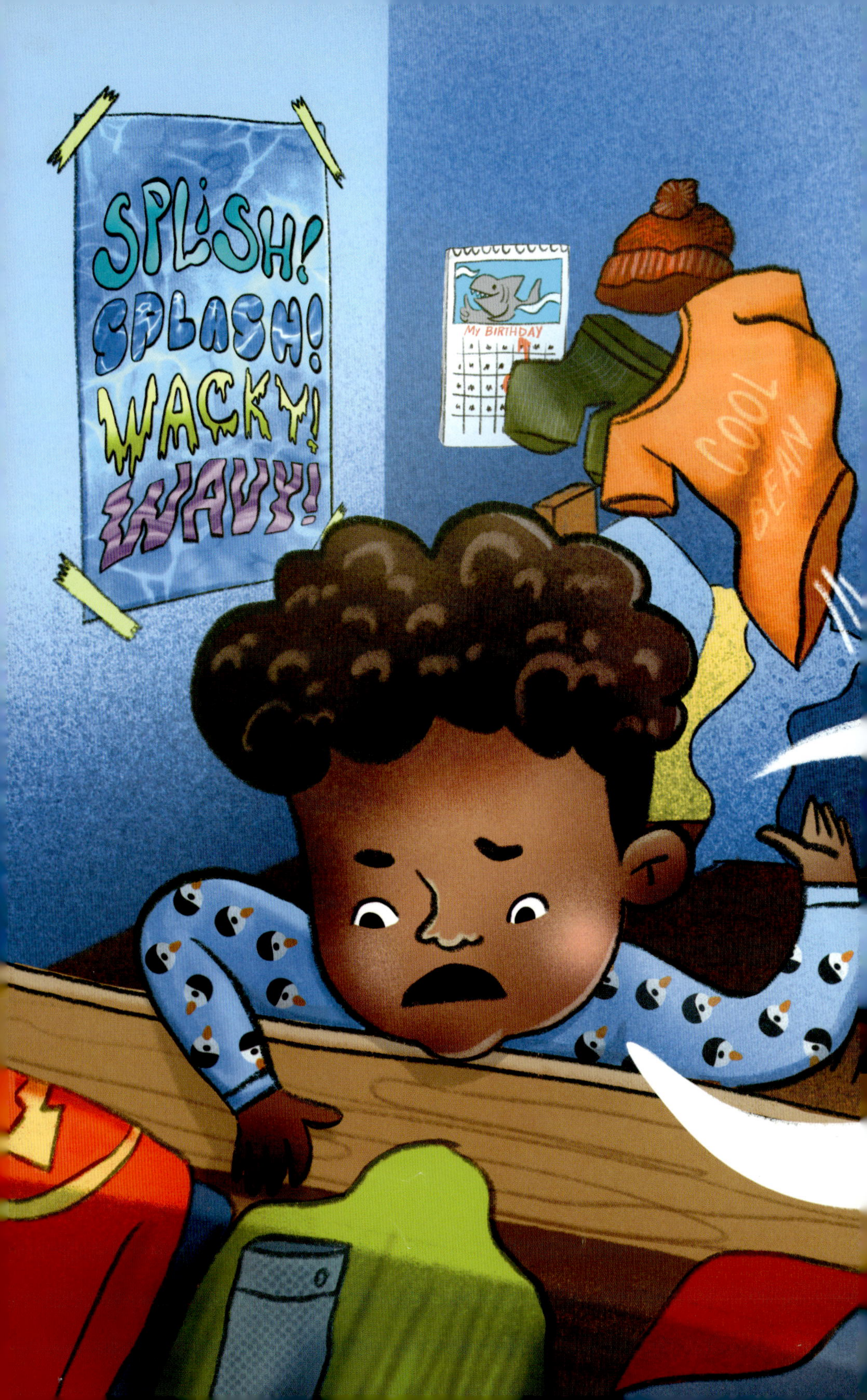
SPLISH!
SPLASH!
WACKY!
WAVY!
MY BIRTHDAY
COOL BEAN

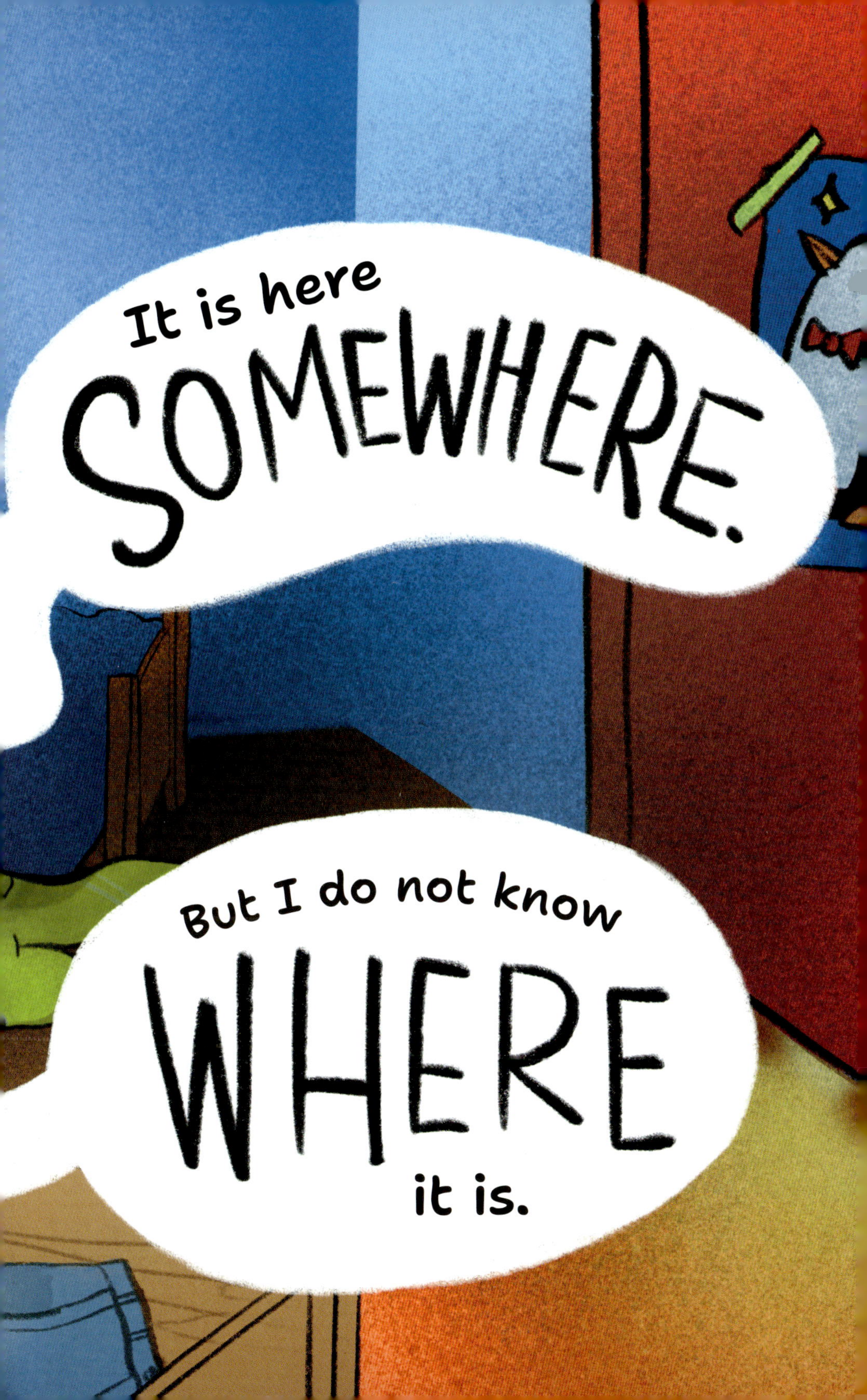
It is here SOMEWHERE.
But I do not know WHERE it is.

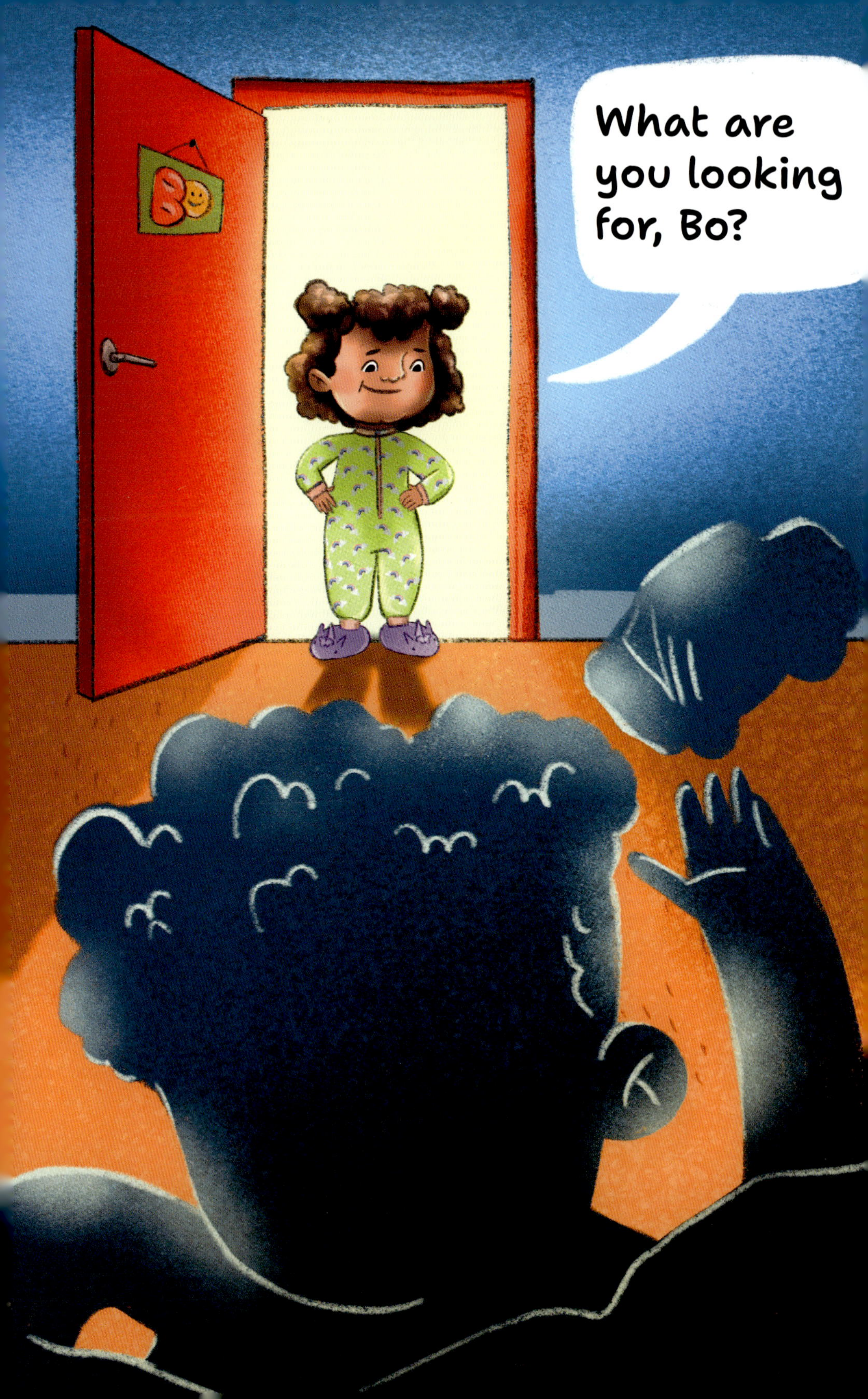
Bo
What are you looking for, Bo?

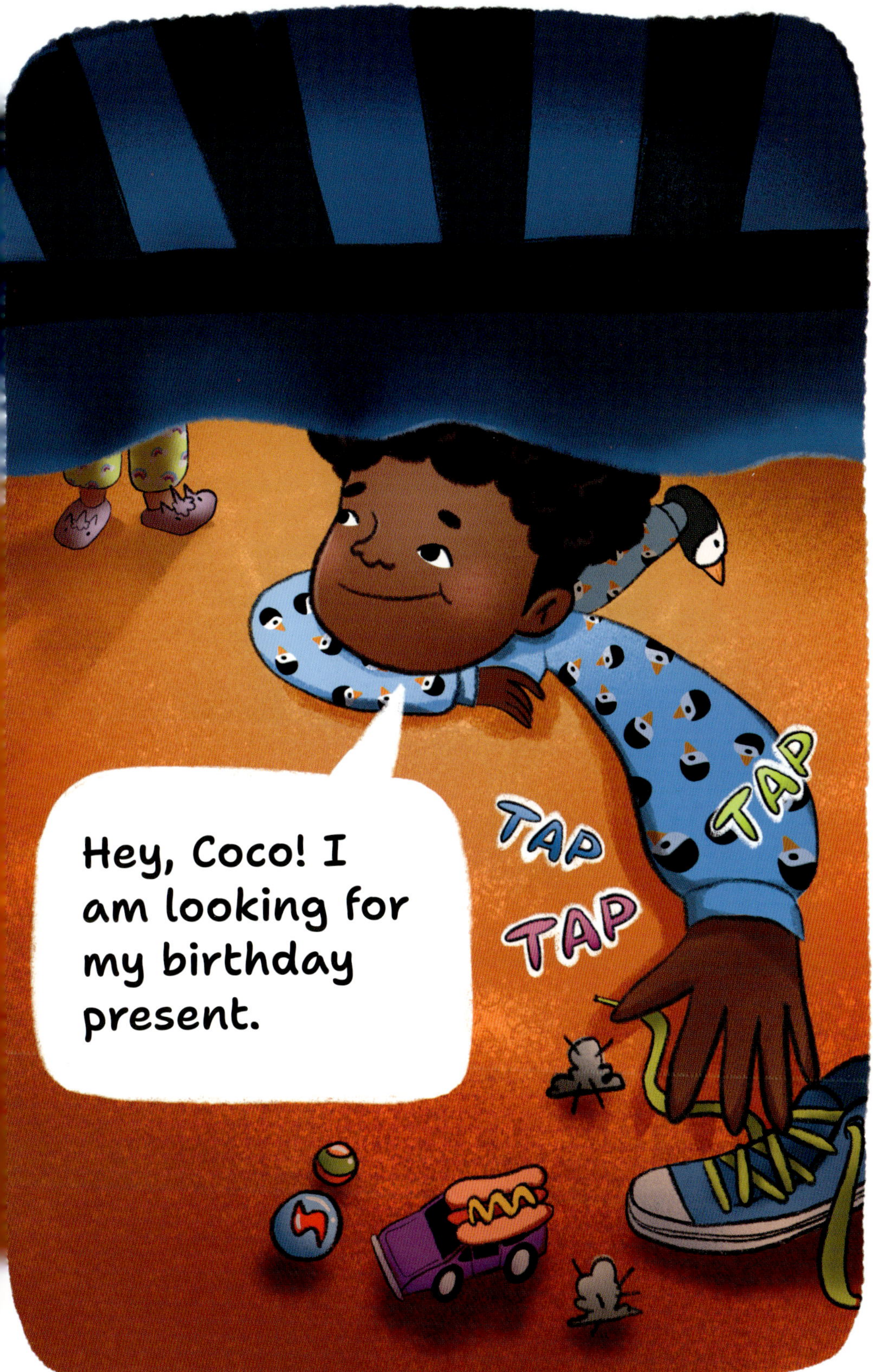
Hey, Coco! I am looking for my birthday present.
TAP
TAP
TAP

Do you really think it is in your dirty clothes hamper?

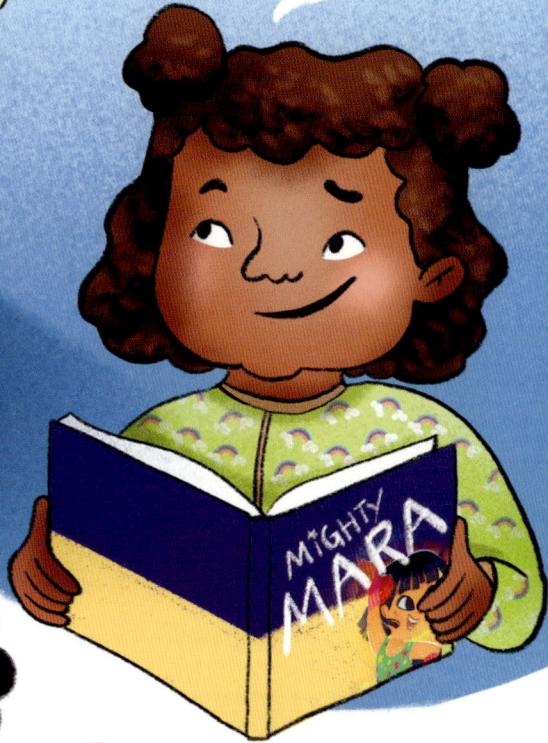

Every year, Mom and Dad hide it somewhere in the house.

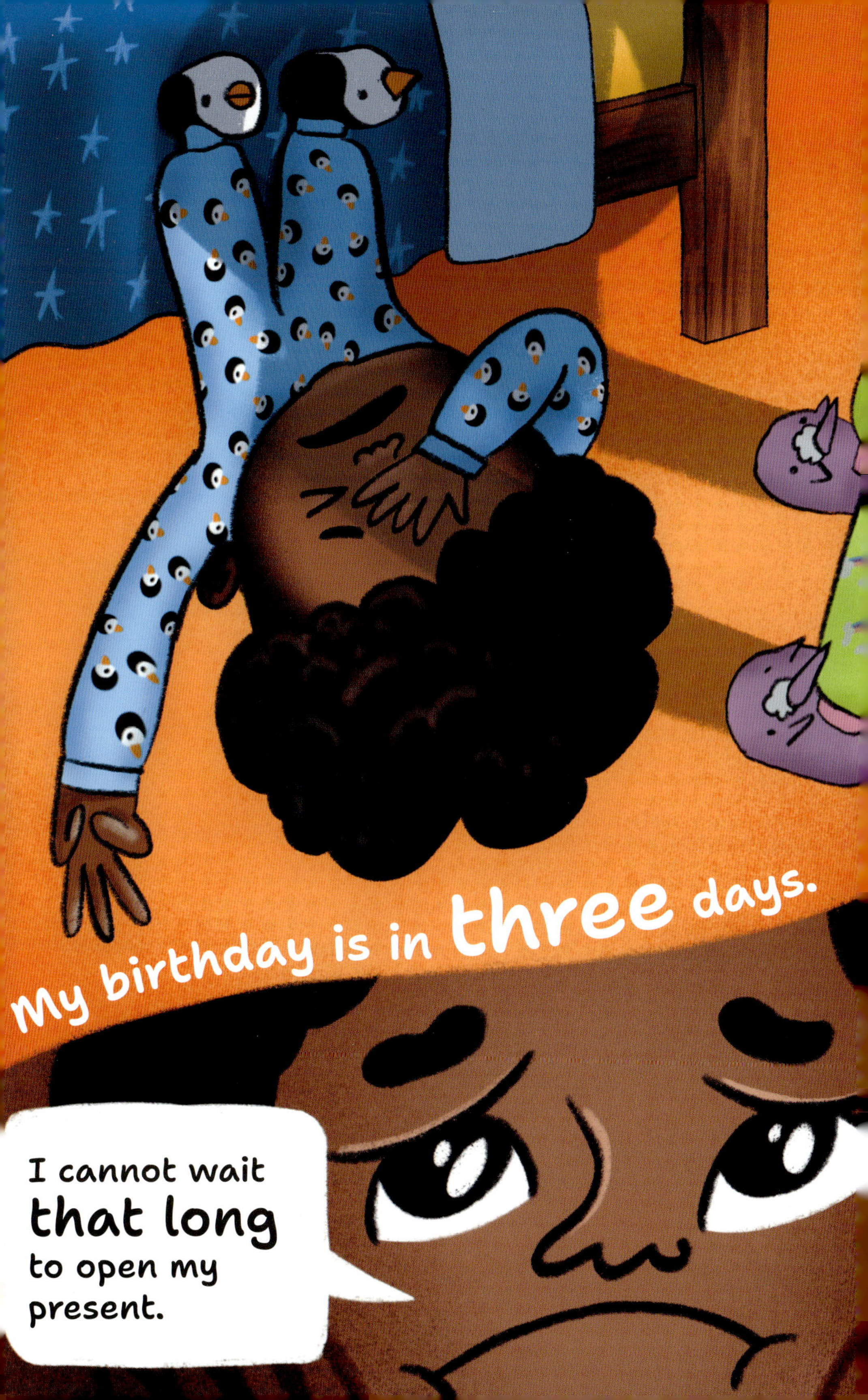
My birthday is in three days.
I cannot wait that long to open my present.

Coco, you are good at finding things. Will you help me find my present?
Of course, Bo! This will be fun.
My first question is...
Where are Mom and Dad's favorite places to hide when we play hide-and-seek?

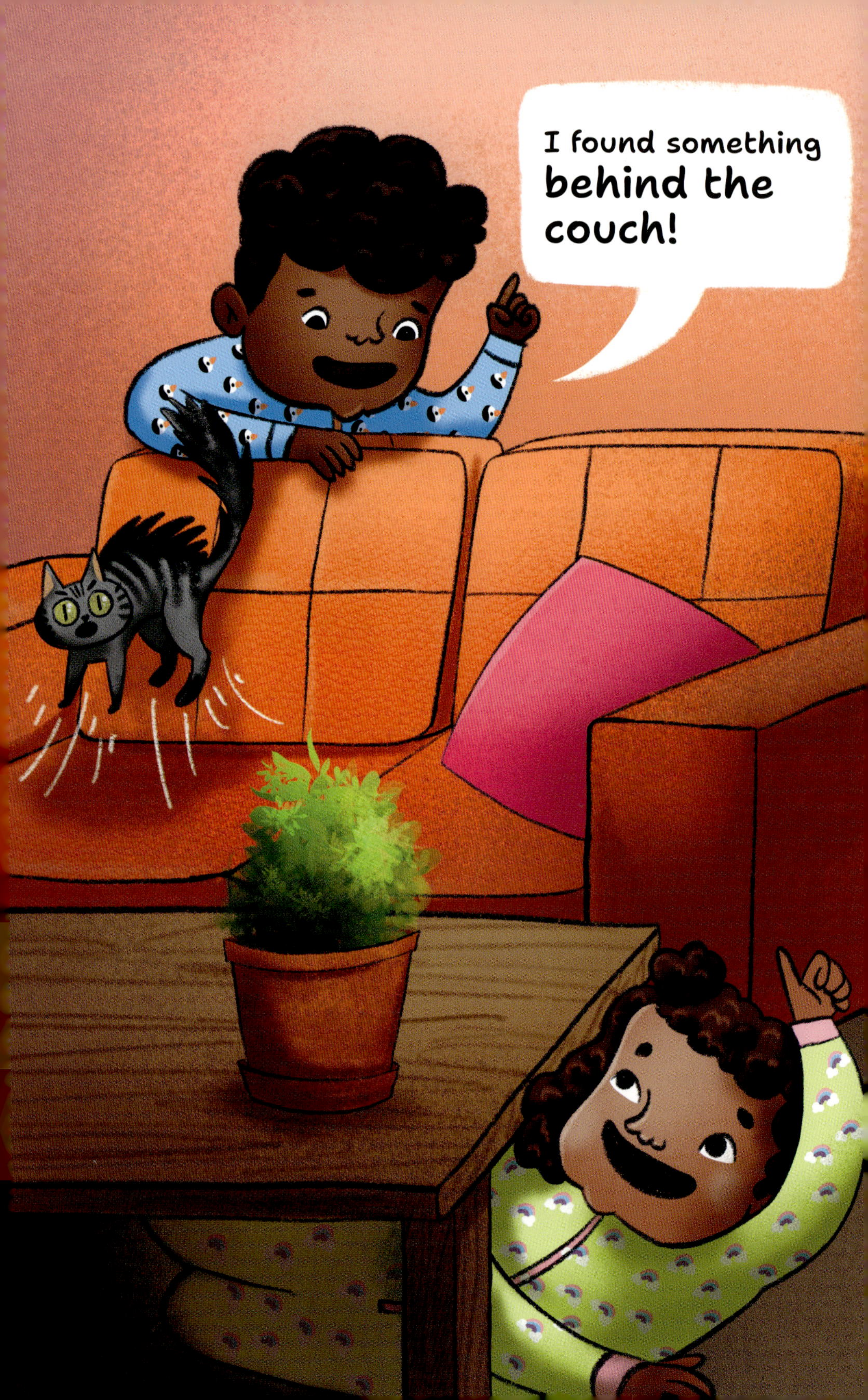
I found something behind the couch!

It is a piece of red ribbon.
Mom and Dad use red ribbon...
TO WRAP PRESENTS!
Great work, Bo!

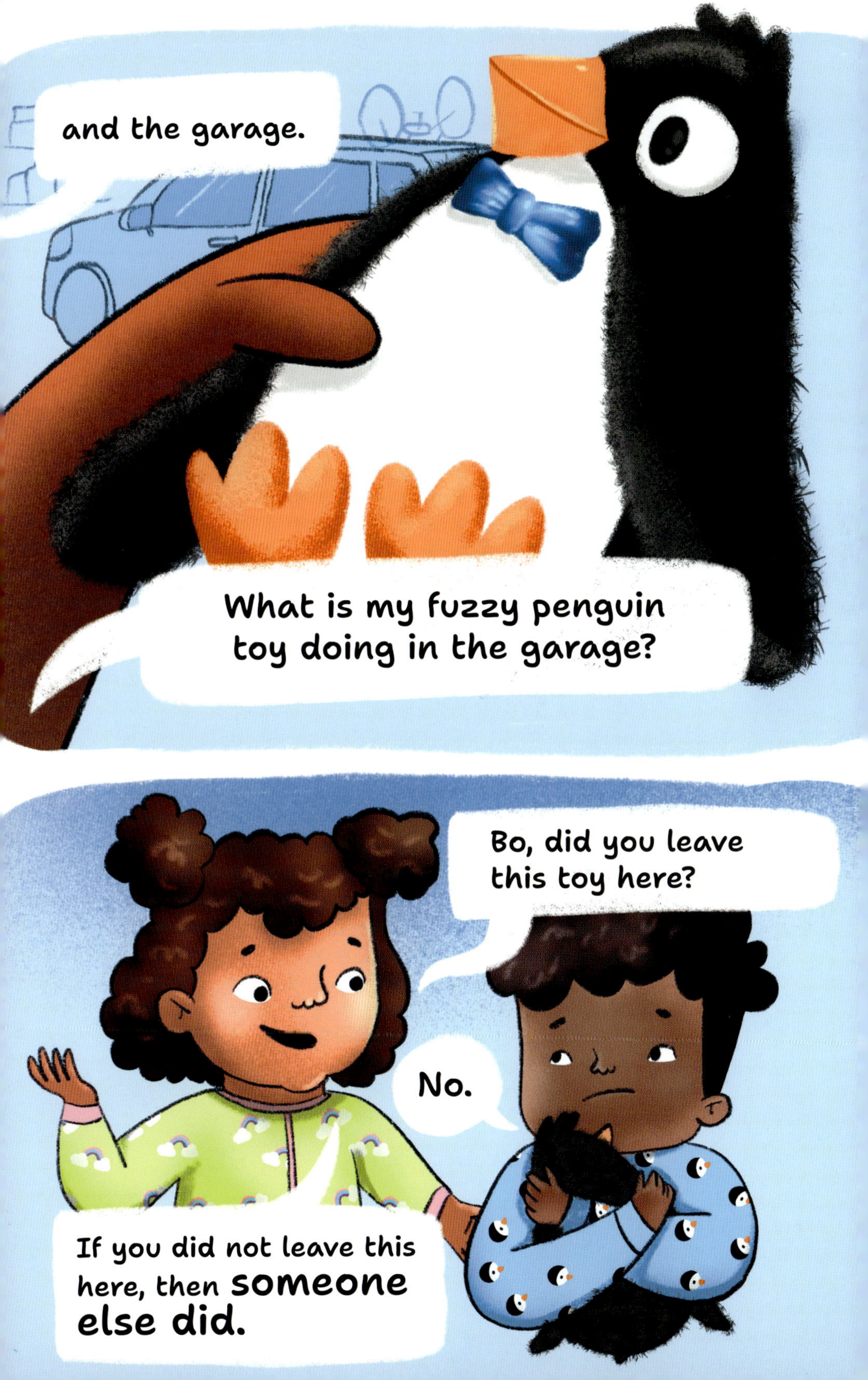
and the garage.
What is my fuzzy penguin toy doing in the garage?
Bo, did you leave this toy here?
No.
If you did not leave this here, then **someone else did.**

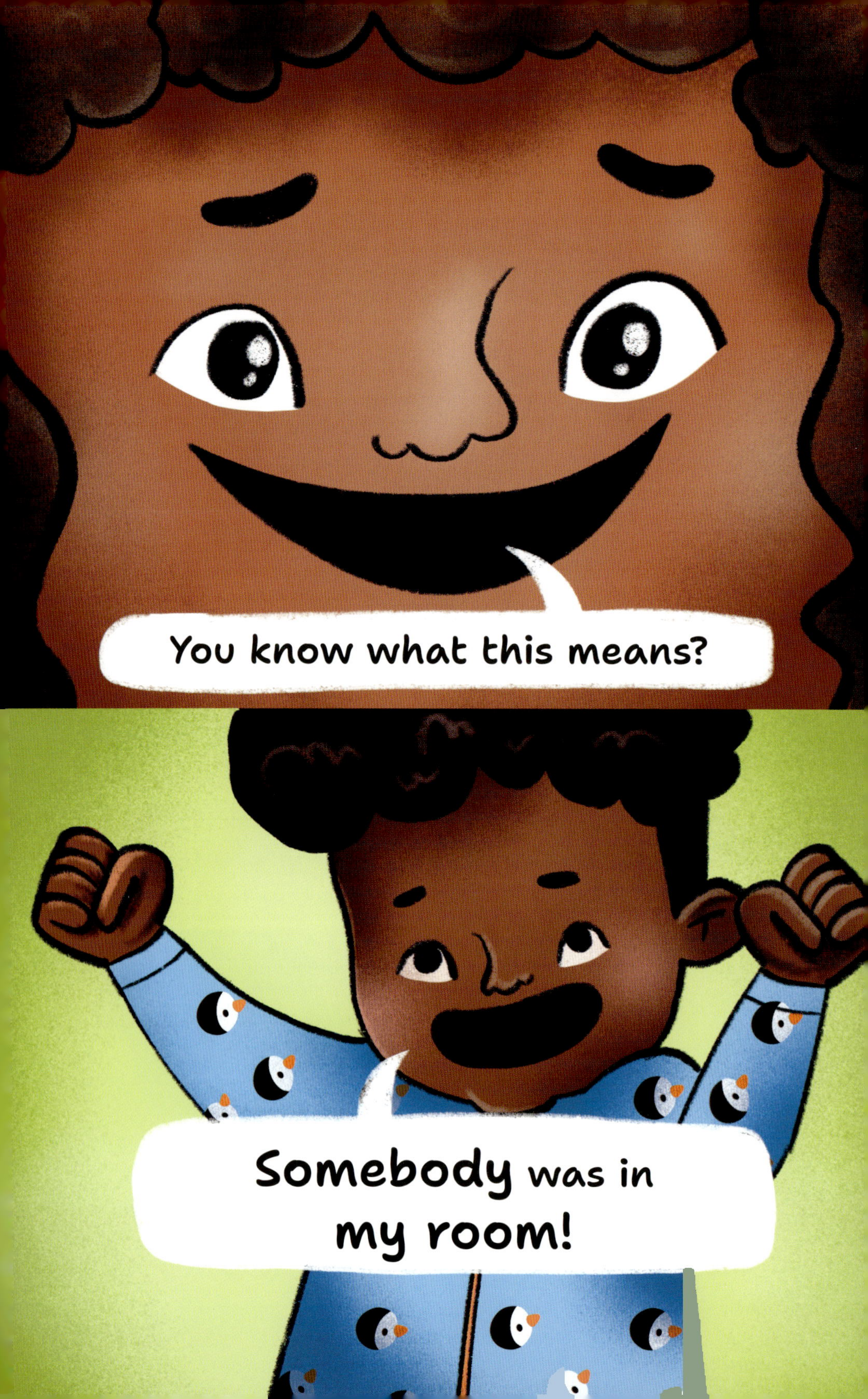
You know what this means?
Somebody was in my room!

Hmm. I think I have my third question.
Where in your room do you keep this fuzzy penguin toy?
The same place I keep all my toys.
In my...

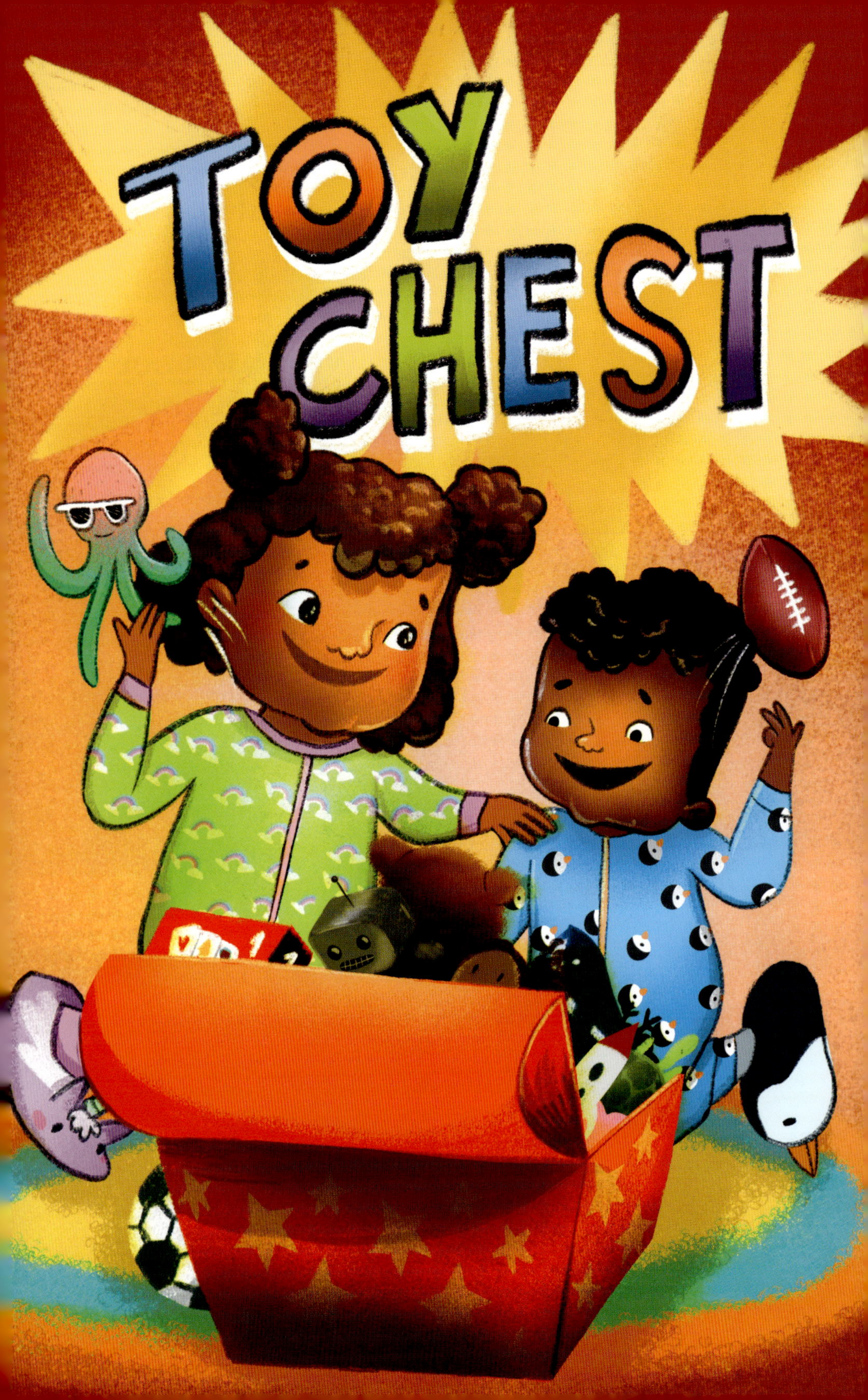
TOY CHEST

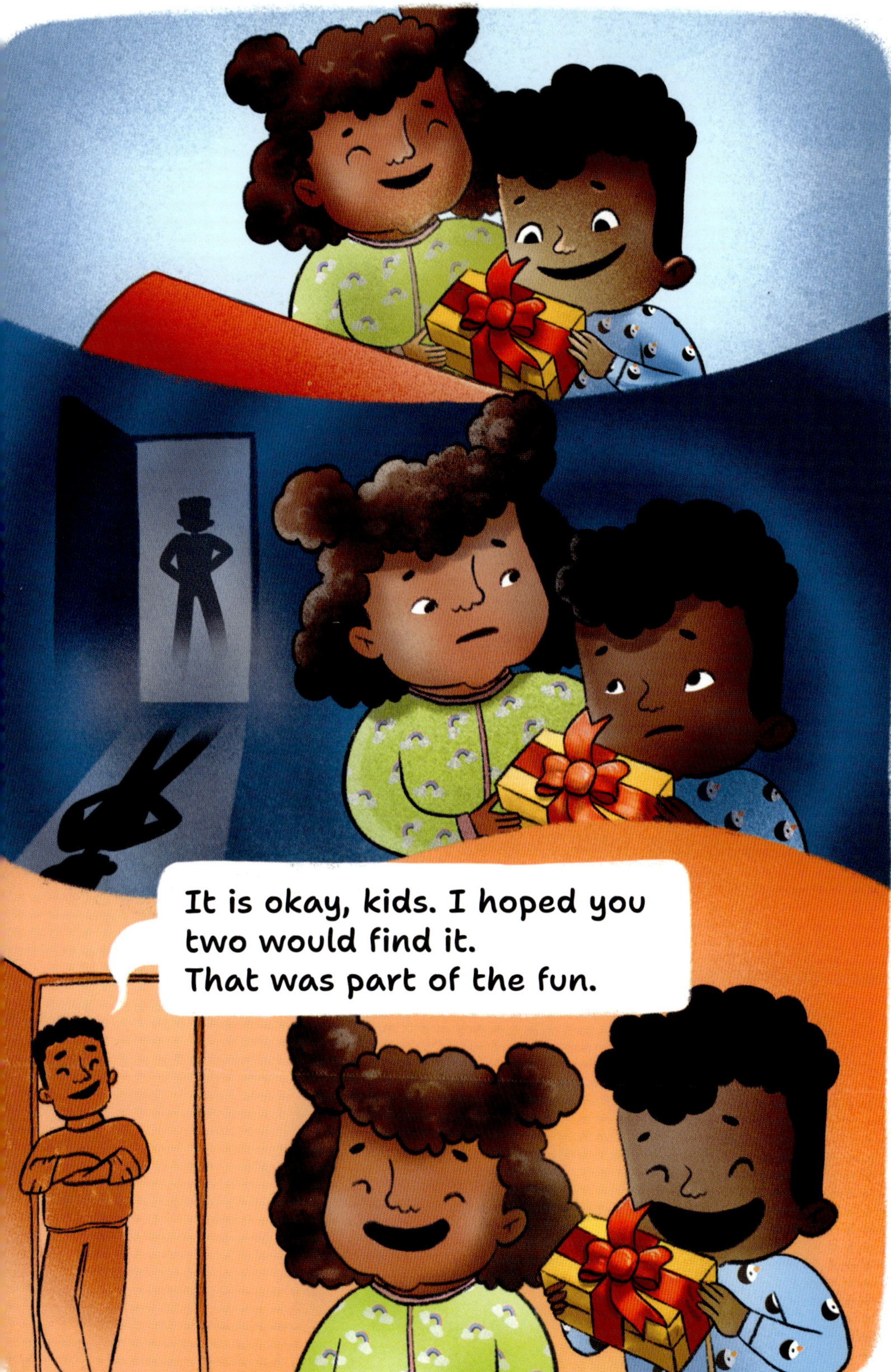
It is okay, kids. I hoped you
two would find it.
That was part of the fun.

2.

What Should We Bring?

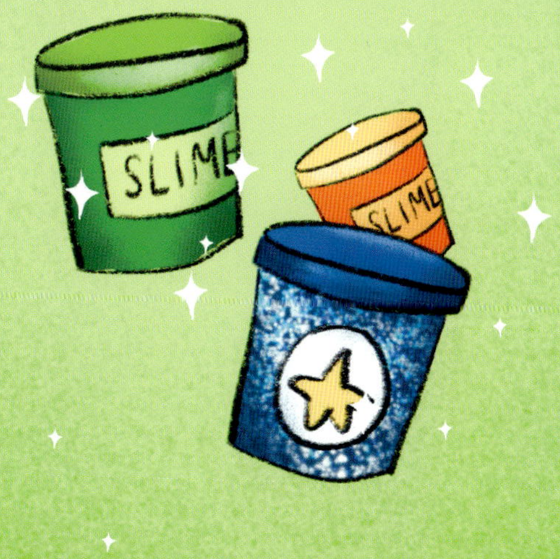
SLIME
SLIME

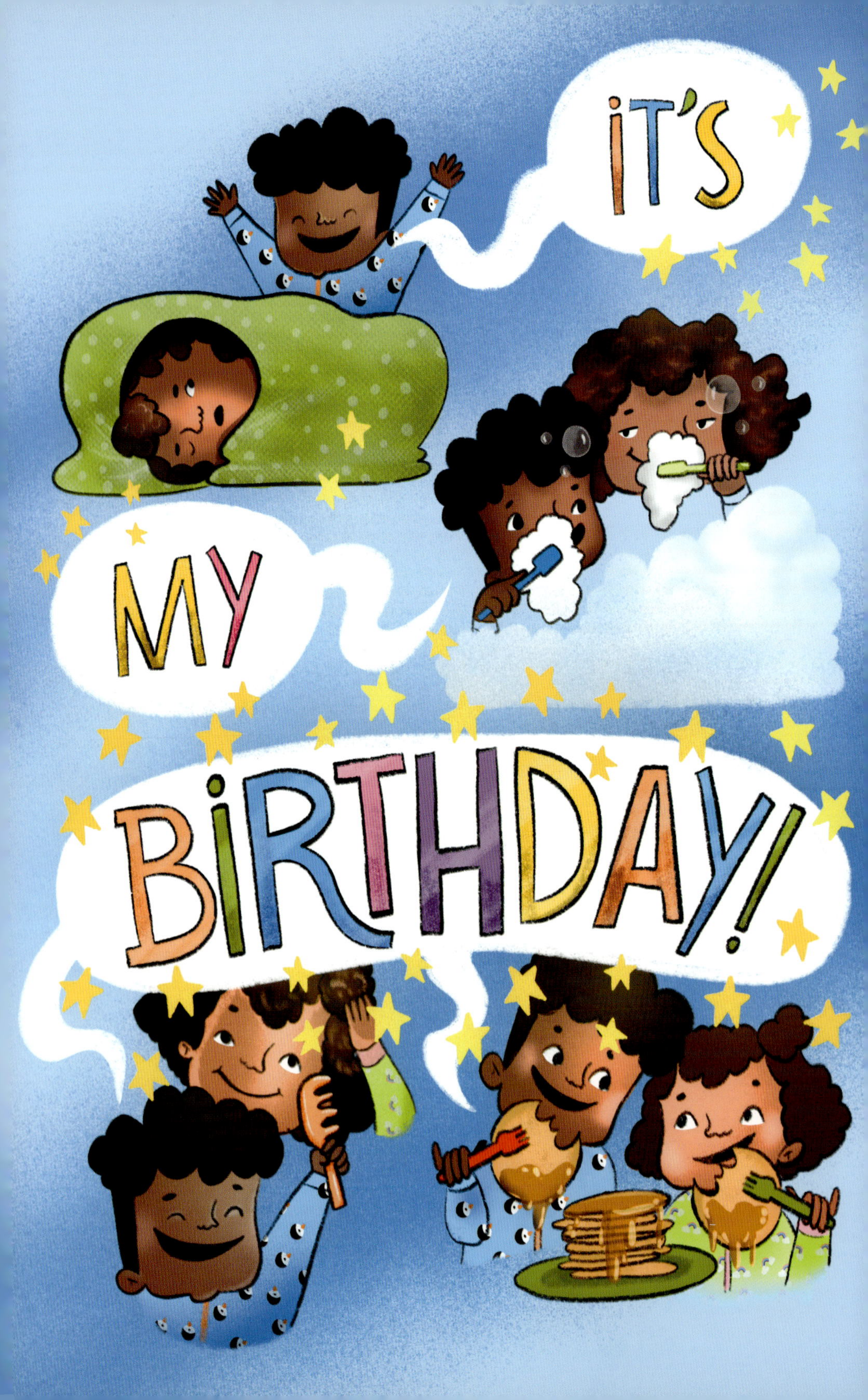
IT'S
MY
BIRTHDAY!

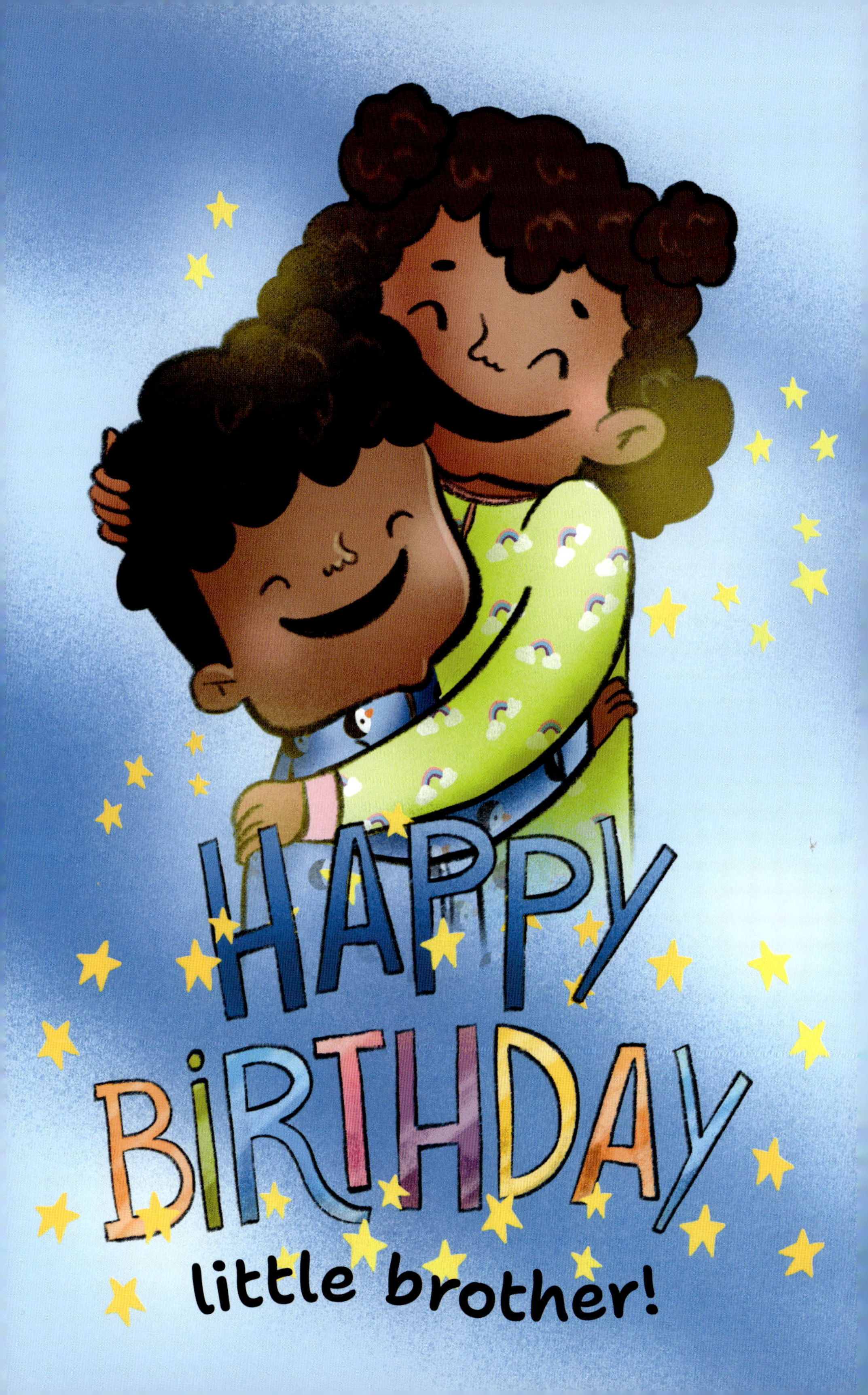
HAPPY
BIRTHDAY
little brother!

We are going to SPLISH! SPLASH!

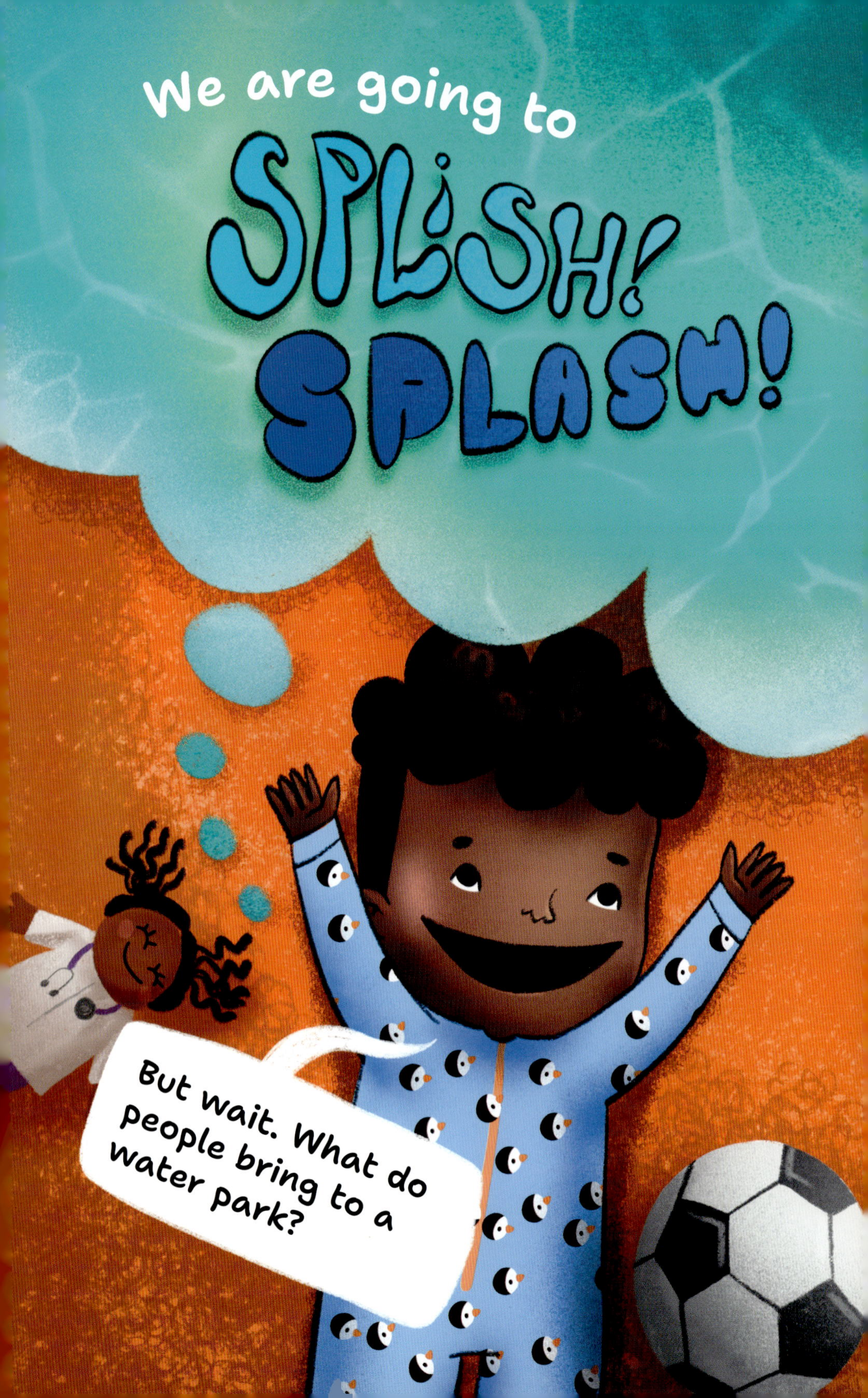
But wait. What do people bring to a water park?

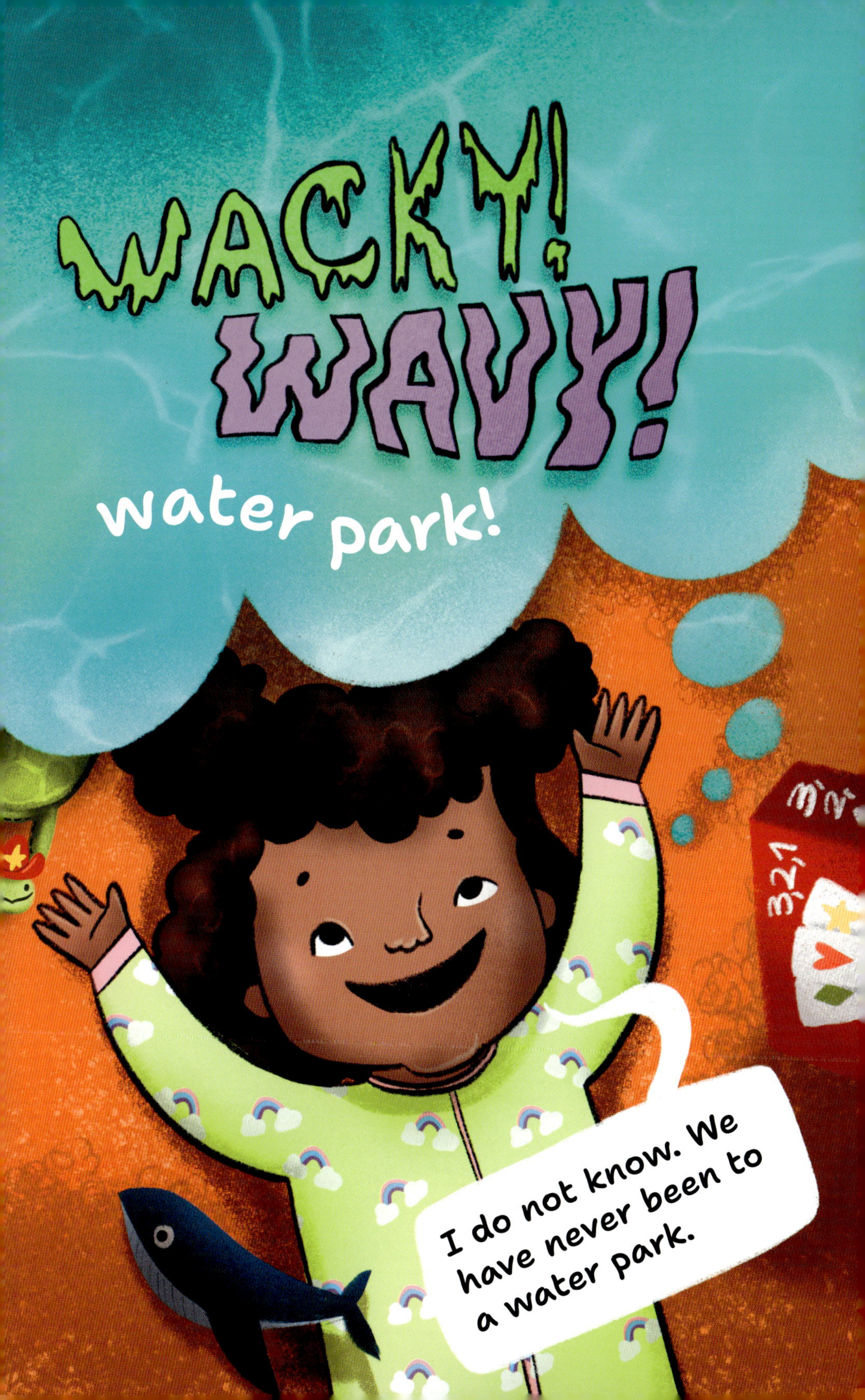

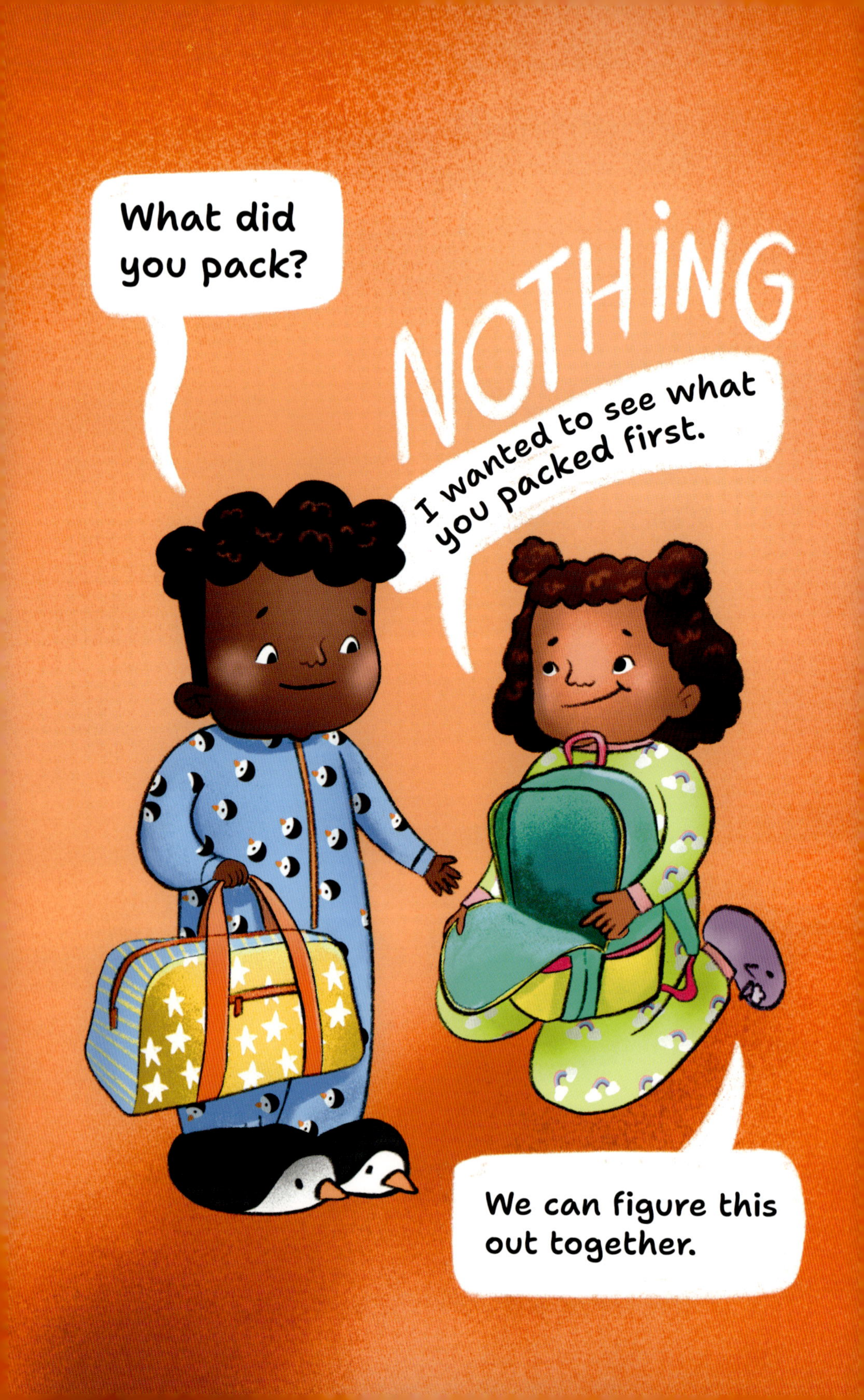
What did you pack?
NOTHING
I wanted to see what you packed first.
We can figure this out together.

Will you bring your stuffed lion?
Maybe stuffed animals are not so good for the water park.

These thing-a-ma-boops?
Hi
Yes! Swimming goggles help me see underwater.

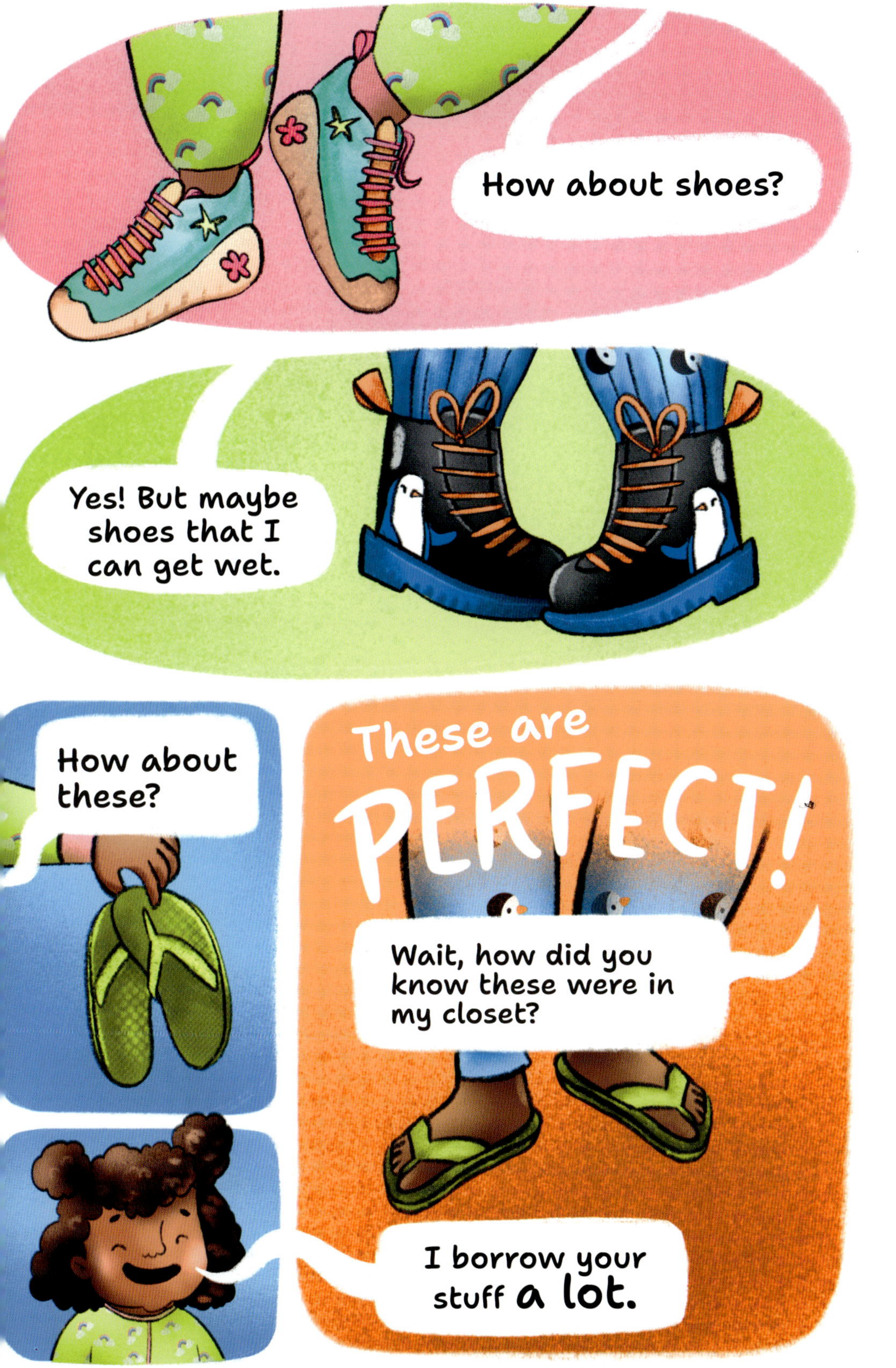
How about shoes?
Yes! But maybe shoes that I can get wet.
How about these?
These are PERFECT!
Wait, how did you know these were in my closet?
I borrow your stuff a lot.

3.

Which Slide Should We Ride?

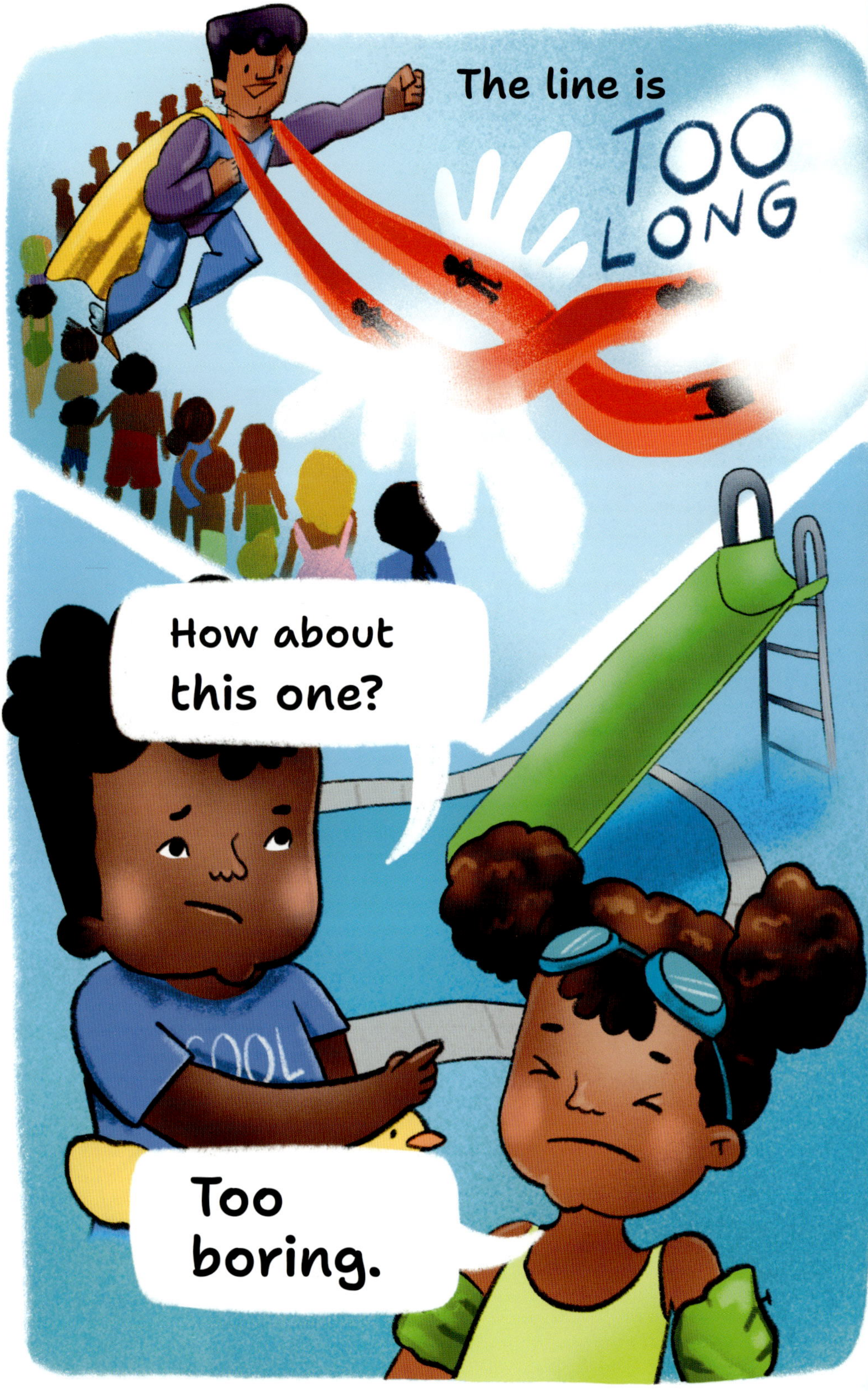

The line is
TOO LONG
How about this one?
COOL
Too
boring.

Wait, I see a winner!
THAT ONE
The really REALLY big one?
Yes. It does not have a long line and it looks fun.
Okay. If you say it looks fun, I will try it.

What if this slide is too fast?
Or too slow?
Or too bendy?
Or too dark?

Bo, are you nervous about going down the slide?
A LITTLE
Wait. More than a little.
You do not have to go down if you do not want to.
We can try another slide and have fun.
No. I want to at least **try** this one.
Okay. How about if I go first?

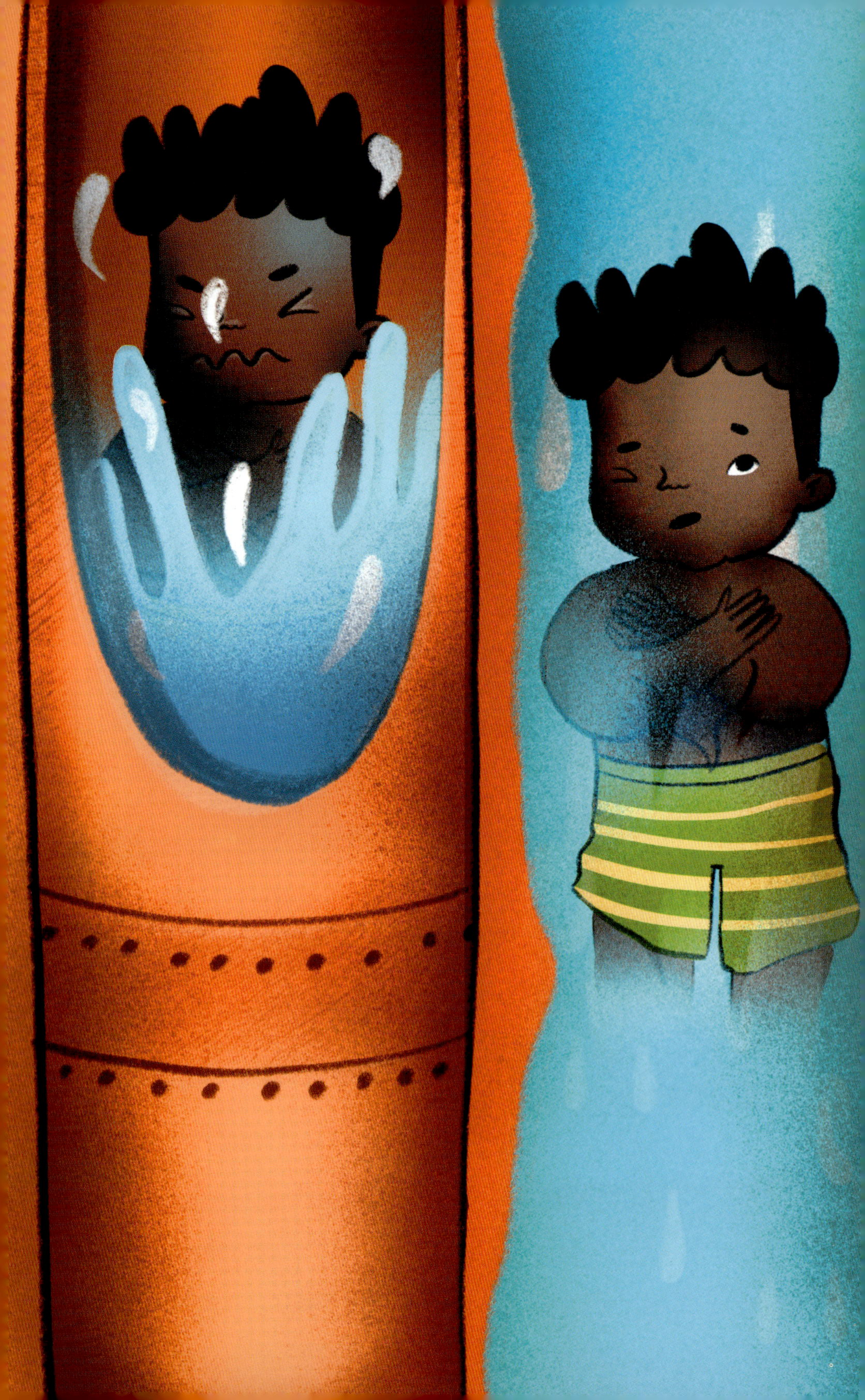

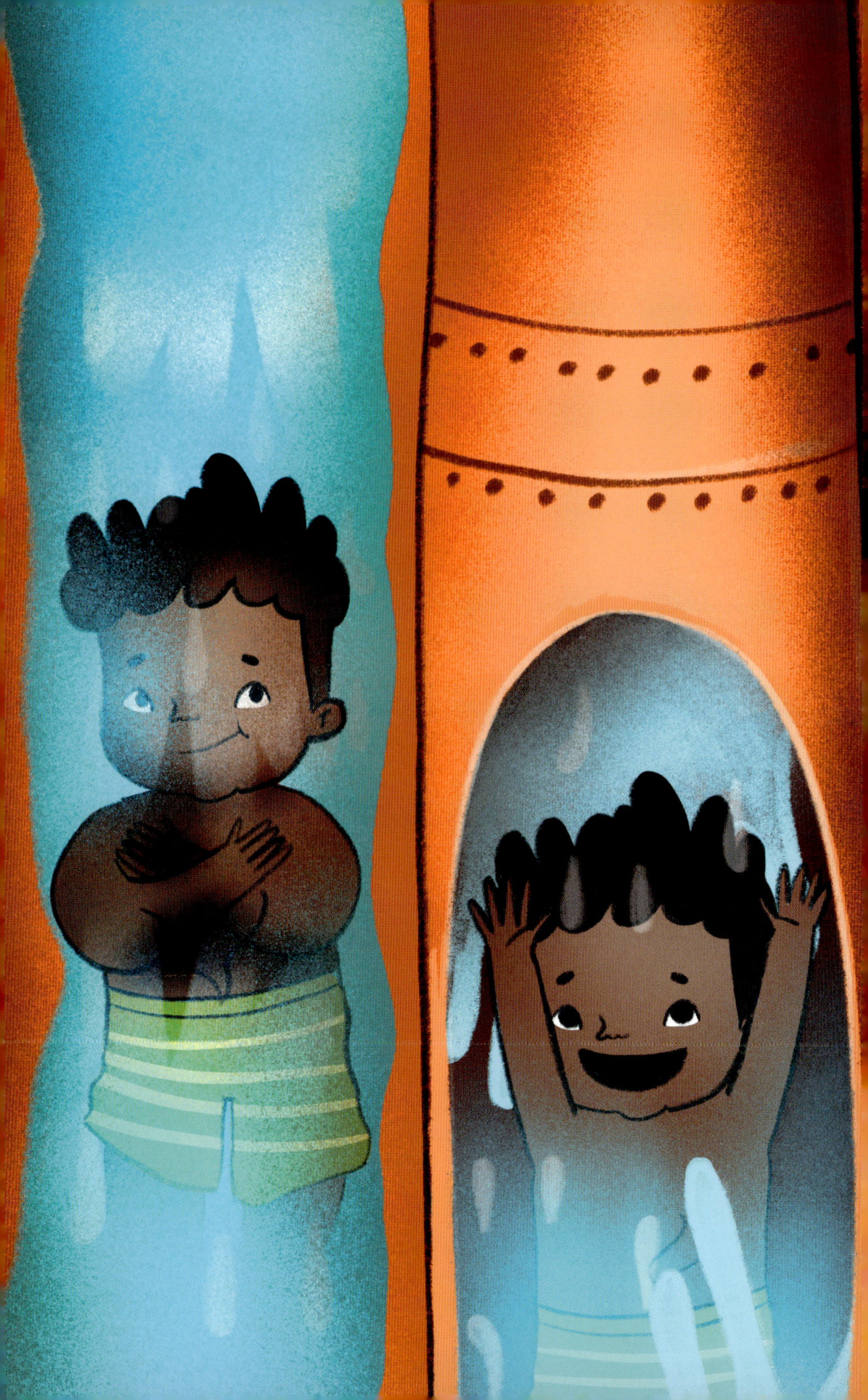

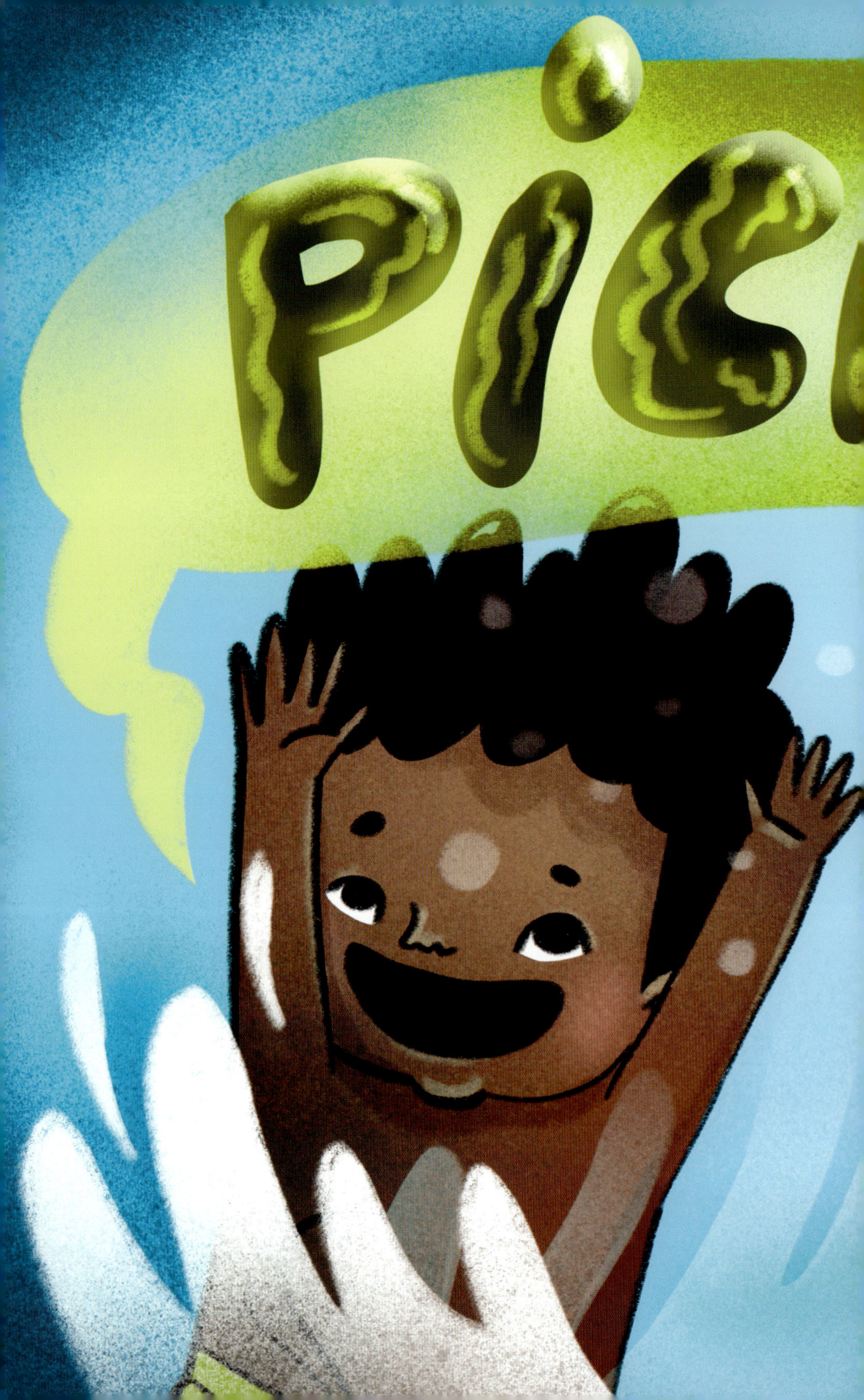
Pic

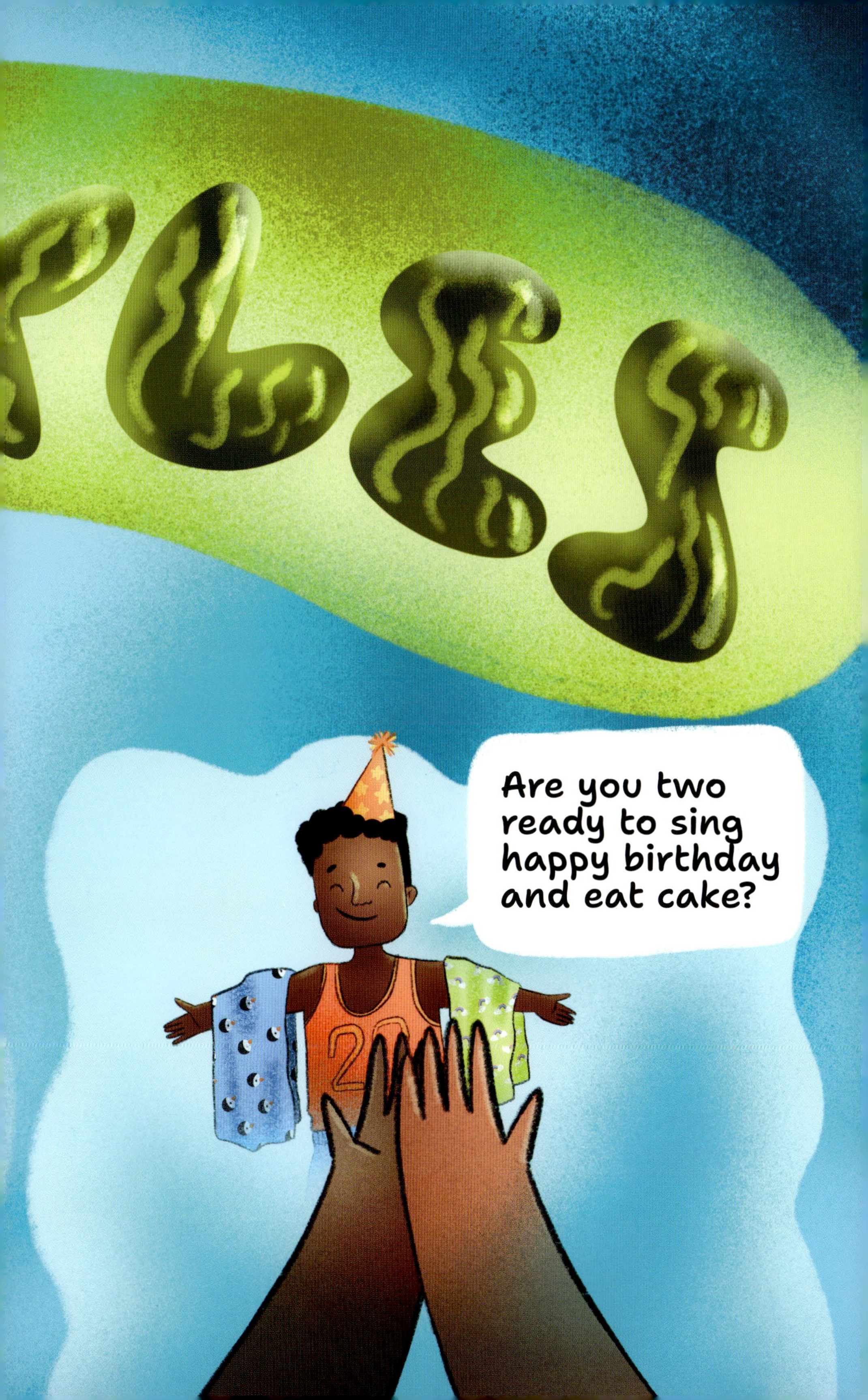
Are you two ready to sing happy birthday and eat cake?

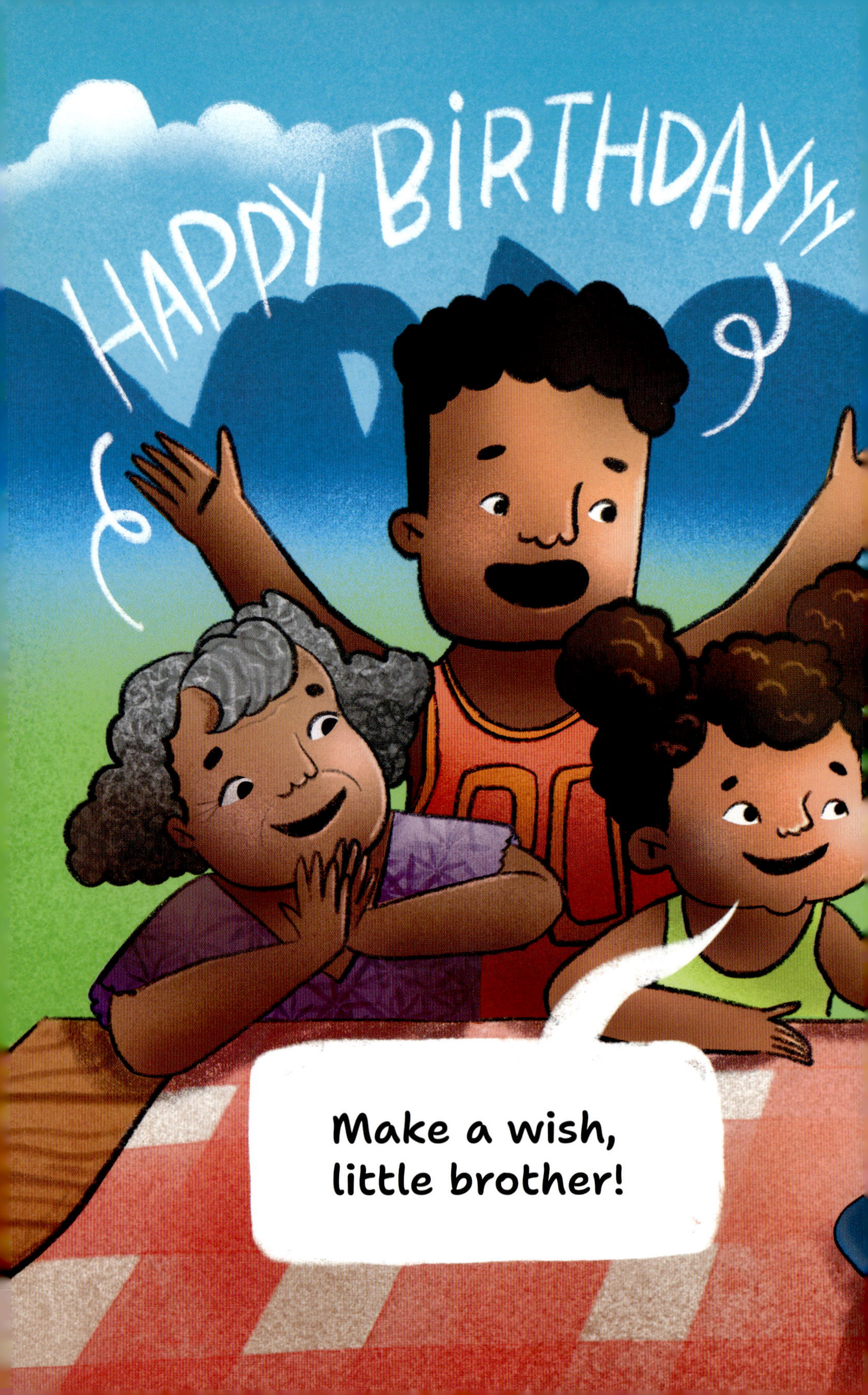
HAPPY BiRTHDAYyy
Make a wish,
little brother!

JESSE BYRD

The most important thing to know about Jesse is that he's an older brother who loves to mess with his younger brother. Bad jokes. Tussling. Aggravating him until he gets a reaction. In this work, Jesse considers himself an artiste.

When he's not doing that (and he does that a lot), he's probably creating stories for young readers.

LAU MORAITI
pronounced "more-eye-tee"

Lau has been a big sister for almost all her life. She loves to play board games whenever her brother visits. As kids, they enjoyed battling at Guess Who? and games of cards.

Lau is an artist from Uruguay, a tiny country in South America. She's a mom who loves to draw stories for kids.

She also loves the color pink, eating pizza, and having many pets.

Use the hashtag **#bigsistercoco** to share YOUR favorite things to do with your siblings!